Laurie Halse Anderson

THE BIG CHEESE of THIRD STREET

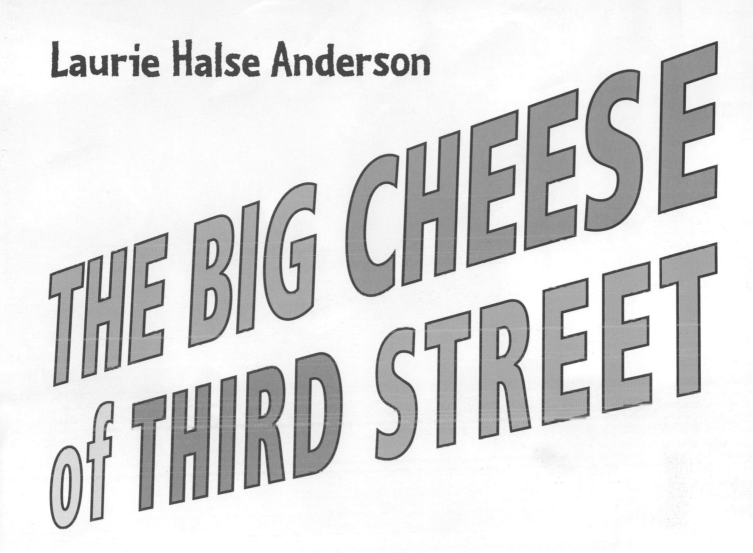

illustrated by
David Gordon

Simon & Schuster Books for Young Readers
New York   London   Toronto   Sydney   Singapore

To my little sister,
Lisa Ellen Halse Stevens, with all my love
—L. H. A.

To my dearest Tatiana
and special thanks to Kevin and Alyssa
—D. G.

SIMON & SCHUSTER BOOKS FOR YOUNG READERS
An imprint of Simon & Schuster Children's Publishing Division
1230 Avenue of the Americas, New York, New York 10020
Text copyright © 2002 by Laurie Halse Anderson
Illustrations copyright © 2002 by David Gordon
Book design by Anahid Hamparian
The text of this book is set in 23-point Kosmik.
The illustrations are rendered in cell vinyl and pencil.

Printed in Hong Kong
2 4 6 8 10 9 7 5 3 1

Library of Congress Cataloging-in-Publication Data
Anderson, Laurie Halse.
The Big Cheese of Third Street / by Laurie Halse Anderson ; illustrated by David Gordon. — 1st ed.
p.   cm.
Summary: Little Benny, no bigger than a peanut butter sandwich,
is the victim of his larger peers until he wins the pole climb at the Third Street block party.
ISBN 0-689-82464-5 (hardcover)
[1. Size—Fiction.] I. Gordon, David, ill. II. Title.
PZ7.H16675Bi 2000
[Fic]—dc21
98-47943

The Big Antonellis and their Big Friends lived on Third Street.

Bus-sized women. Skyscraper-sized men.
Kids taller than streetlights.
    Except for Little Benny—The Tiny Antonelli.

He was no bigger than a peanut butter sandwich.

The Big Antonelli Kids loved to play with Little Benny.
They stuffed him into snowballs.
They taped him to toy airplanes.
They even made him walk the dogs.

"Help!" hollered Little Benny.

When the Antonellis played keep-away with the Sorensons of Second Street, Little Benny got to be the ball.
"Put me down!" shouted Little Benny.

When the Antonellis and the Sorensons played sharks at the pool,
Little Benny got to be the minnow.
"Let me out of here!" squeaked Little Benny.

Being small was no fun. Little
Benny wanted to hang out with
the Big Kids. But mostly he just
hung on.

After a while Little Benny learned to stay out of the way. He shinnied up street signs. He crawled up fire escapes. He climbed fences and trees, drainpipes and telephone poles.

The Big Kids chased, and Little Benny climbed. And that was life on Third Street.

Well, that was life until the day of the annual Third Street block party.

3RD ST
BLOCK
PARTY
FUN!
FOOD!
GAMES

We're talking about the best block party in the world, here. You got your games, you got your food, you got your music. But best of all, you got your greased pole climb. And whoever took the cheese from the top of that slippery, slimy pole, that person would be the hero of Third Street.

The whole neighborhood banged, clanged, and cooked in preparation.

But what about Little Benny?

His day didn't start out so good. He went out back to play, and his worst sister pinned him to the clothesline along with the Big Antonelli underpants.

"Rats," said Little Benny.
He unpinned himself and swung down on a gym sock.

He went out front to play, and Enormous Norman Antonelli swept him into a dustpan and dumped him in the trash.

"Yuck, ptooey," coughed Little Benny.
He climbed up a cereal box and jumped to the ground.

EATS

Now, Little Benny, he was used to this sort of stuff. Happened all the time. But then Big June Warren chased him down, dressed him in doll clothes, and stuck him in her stroller. That was the last straw.

"This stinks," muttered Little Benny.

He snuck out of the stroller, ditched the dress, and raced across the picnic table, only to be snagged by Big Aunt Eulalie, who thought he was a tomato.

She tossed him into a salad bowl with the onions and olives.

Little Benny felt lower than gum stuck to the sidewalk. Lower than pigeon poop. Lower than worm guts. Pretty low.

That's when the nasty Sorensons of Second Street rumbled over.

The Biggest Sorenson bumped bellies with the Biggest Antonelli.

"We challenge you to the pole climb," shouted the Sorenson.
"First one to the top gets the cheese," answered the Antonelli.

The two teams took turns.

An Antonelli wrapped his arms around the pole, pulled himself up, and slid right back down.

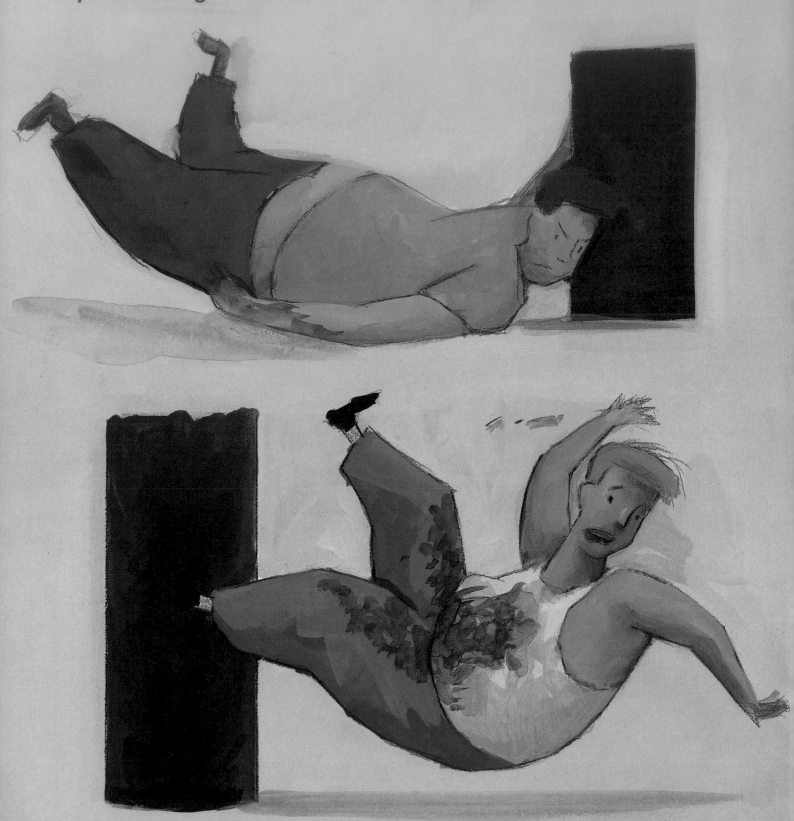

Then a Sorenson climbed hand-over-hand, got two feet off the ground, and crashed back to Earth.

The pole was as slippery as butter on a hot stove. The Antonellis jumped. The Sorensons leaped. Up they went. Down they plunged. **NOTHING** worked.

"What a bunch of yutzes," said Little Benny. "They can't climb. They can't hang on for nothing. They'll never get to the top."

The street filled with sweat. The cheese, prize of all prizes, waited at the tippy-top of the pole, as far away as the moon. Not one Antonelli or Sorenson could reach it. Not one.

Until Little Benny walked up and put his tiny hand on the pole.

The block party stopped for a minute, and everybody stared. Little Benny? Climb the pole? He's too small to do anything!

Everybody roared with laughter.
Antonellis cackled.
Sorensons guffawed.
What a joke!

Little Benny's ears burned. He wanted to cry. He studied the pole and found a good place for his hand. Then he started up.

Right hand, left foot, pull, hold on. He didn't weigh too much, so he didn't slide down.

Left hand, right foot, pull. Up he went. Higher and higher.

Right hand, left foot, pull.

The laughter below faded. His ears popped. Beneath him, the city started to look like a sandbox town. The streets were straight lines drawn with a stick, the river a crooked stripe of blue. Itty-bitty dockworkers unloaded a ship.

Office buildings stood no bigger than bricks.

The Third Street block party swirled like a box of melted crayons.
The ant-sized Antonellis and the gnat-sized Sorensons looked up
at him.

Soon the cheese hung just above Benny's head.

Did he go
for it?

Of course he did! Geeeesh, what did you think this story was about?

He reached out, grabbed the cheese, and slid down the pole fast as lightning.

The crowd went nuts—badda-boom, badda-bing—the kid gets a new name.
  Little Benny Antonelli—

The Big Cheese of Third Street